IN MEMORIAM

Louis Travis Branch

My gratitude, honor, and love go toward my father who served God and country in the

US Coast Guard and later became a judge in the city of Virginia Beach.

Earl Leo Snyder

I have the utmost respect for my father-in-law who served in the US Navy for 32 years.

He and my mother- in-law were laid to rest in Arlington National

Cemetery. We had a kinship as he, too, was an artist.

- Melissa Branch Snyder

DEDICATION

To my niece and nephews, Scarlett, Titus, and James.

As the children of a military family, there are so many goodbyes. You three are writing

a new chapter to your story with every move you make. I wrote this book with you all in the

forefront of my heart and mind. No matter where you are in the world, I carry you with me.

Thank you for being the unsung heroes of this Nation and for the sacrifices you make

alongside your Mommy and Daddy every single day. This book is for you.

- Coco

This book is given with love

 **To**

_____

 **From**

_____

American Dream Team

★ A Kid's Guide to Patriotism ★

By Courtney Petruzzelli

Illustrated by Melissa B. Snyder

The Declaration was signed. The message sent.

Truths undeniable, self-evident.

$\mathcal{H}$eroic men and women fought strong and brave

so that our stars and stripes could forever wave.

Some marched to be equal,

to have the same rights.

Due to their voices,

we can reach the same heights!

Some serve and protect, at home or away.

Their acts of valor put freedom on display.

$\mathscr{B}$ut, independence comes with a price.

For some made the ultimate sacrifice.

*O*n several occasions throughout the year,

we show respect to those who carried us here.

The Fourth of July, Veterans, and Memorial Day...

are more than just fireworks and their brilliant display.

It's a time to remember, salute and honor,

America's finest and our Nation's forefathers.

It's a time in our life where we can lend a hand;

And listen, not speak, so we can understand.

To soldiers of young and soldiers of old

who fought for our freedoms, fearless and bold.

$\mathcal{T}$his year let us do something great;

a special tradition to honor these dates.

No matter your age - if you're too young to vote -

gratitude is a cause we ALL can promote.

Lady Liberty is ready to hand off her torch.

Let's start with a thank you on a hero's porch...

$\mathcal{A}$ flag, a gift, a hug, a card...

or time out of the day to show your regard.

These acts of kindness will make someone's day.

The American Dream Team is on the way!

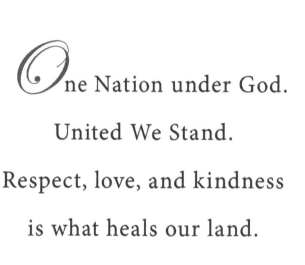

One Nation under God.

United We Stand.

Respect, love, and kindness

is what heals our land.

"Land of the free!," our leaders all say,

with hope that tomorrow, you'll lead the way.

Be proud, young Patriot, for you are part of the team,

where every day we celebrate the American dream.

God Bless America!

Love Thy Neighbor:
A Hero's Call

Ask your family these questions to start your own American Dream Team tradition:

Dear Veteran,
Thank you for serving and protecting our country.
♥ Amy
USA ☺

⭐ Who is a hero in your life?

⭐ What is a way that you can thank him or her?

⭐ What does it mean to you to be a hero?

⭐ What does it mean to you to be an American?

⭐ How can you make a difference in your community?

Claim Your FREE Gift!

 Visit:

PDICBooks.com/Gift

Thank you for purchasing

American Dream Team

and welcome to the Puppy Dogs & Ice Cream family.
We're certain you're going to love the little gift
we've prepared for you at the website above.

Printed in the USA
CPSIA information can be obtained
at www.ICGtesting.com
LVHW071341251023
761977LV00004B/5